Dreams and Death in African Mythology: The History of Legends and Folk Stories about Dreams and Death across Africa

By Charles River Editors

A picture of an early 20th century Yoruba divination board

About Charles River Editors

Charles River Editors is a boutique digital publishing company, specializing in bringing history back to life with educational and engaging books on a wide range of topics. Keep up to date with our new and free offerings with this 5 second sign up on our weekly mailing list, and visit Our Kindle Author Page to see other recently published Kindle titles.

We make these books for you and always want to know our readers' opinions, so we encourage you to leave reviews and look forward to publishing new and exciting titles each week.

Introduction

A picture of Bakonogo masks from Central Africa

In the Lasta Mountains of northern Ethiopia, high on an arid plateau in the foothills, the settlement of Lalibela slumbered for centuries as little more than a pilgrimage site at the end of a long and weary footpath. The ancient trade routes between the Eritrean coast and the central highland redoubts that would later coalesce as the imperial capital of Addis Ababa passed fifty miles to the east of Lalibela, and from the early thirteenth century, after the passing of Gebre Mesqel Lalibela himself, the site slipped into decline. The focus of imperial government shifted south, under the influence of successive emperors, as the holy sites of Roha faded from the popular consciousness. Only the occasional band of pilgrims made the journey over the rugged mountain passes, and across the waterless high valleys to repose at the mythical site, now known only to a handful of faithful acolytes.

The site first came to European attention when it was visited in the early 16th century by the Portuguese explorer Pêro da Covilhã, who struck inland from Zeila on the Somali coast in a quest for the legendary Kingdom of Prester John. He was received by the Emperor Eskender, but he was effectively held a prisoner in Ethiopia for 30 years. During that time, he visited and briefly recorded his impressions of Lalibela.

Also in search of the Kingdom of Prester John was the Portuguese missionary Francisco Álvares, who arrived in Ethiopia in 1515 as part of an ambassadorial mission authorized by the Portuguese King Manuel I. There, in the court of the Emperor Dawit II, he met numerous sundry Europeans, including Pêro da Covilhã, and Nicolò Brancaleon, the Venetian painter who settled in Ethiopia in 1480 and whose artistic influence remains visible in ecclesiastical imagery all over the country.

It was Alvarez who described in detail the monuments of Lalibela in his exhaustive travelogue,

A True Relation of the Lands of Prester John of the Indies. The explorer wrote, "At a day's journey from this church of Imbra Christo are edifices, the like of which and so many, cannot, as it appears to me, be found in the world. They are churches entirely excavated in the rock, very well hewn. The names of these churches are these: Emanuel, St. Saviour, St. Mary, Holy Cross, St. George, Golgotha, Bethlehem, Marcoreos, the Martyrs. The principal one is Lalibela. This Lalibela, they say, was a King in this same country for eighty years, and he was King before the one before mentioned who was named Abraham. This King ordered these edifices to be made. He does not lie in the church which bears his name, he lies in the church of Golgotha, which is the church of the fewest buildings here."

In 1550, an edition of Alvarez's book was published in Venice by Giovanni Battista Ramusio, the Italian geographer and travel writer. This version included numerous drawings and plans, but who supplied these illustrations remains a mystery. The next known European visitor to the site was Miguel de Castanhoso, a low-ranking soldier in the service of Cristóvão da Gama, a Portuguese diplomat and soldier who led an aggressive but ultimately unsuccessful military crusade into Ethiopia between 1541 and 1543. What took Miguel de Castanhoso to Lalibela is not known, nor were his impressions recorded.

By the dawn of the 17th century, Portuguese influence in Africa fell into decline, and the occasions of European contact with Ethiopia became very few and far between. It would be another three centuries before another European would venture into the holy precincts of Lalibela as part of a British military expedition mounted in 1867. Thus, the "rediscovery" of the remarkable churches and the story of Christianity in Ethiopia would only be recently written.

As that indicates, the modern history of Africa was, until very recently, written on behalf of the indigenous races by the white man, who had forcefully entered the continent during a particularly hubristic and dynamic phase of European history. When they began to arrive in sub-Saharan Africa in the early 16th century, Christian missionaries replaced established animist practices with the tenets of Christianity. This was particularly true for the Catholics who offered a faith promising eternal paradise upon the simple confession of sin. In an age of slavery, disease, and inter-tribal warfare when life was unembellished, brutal, and usually short, this was a particularly seductive message. Add to this the ritual inherent in Catholic worship, the drinking of blood and the eating of flesh, and the susceptibilities of a society defined by elaborate religious rituals, and the conversion succeeded with extraordinary ease.

It is also true that the Catholic spiritual hierarchy reflected the structure of African spiritual life. The first line of African worship is composed of the spirits of passed ancestors whose relationship with the living remains direct and active. This overlapped with the idea of a host of saints endowed with specific functions and responsibilities. At a higher level, the more remote ancestral spirits, those of more than three or four generations past who have merged into the overall spirit of the nation, formed a less definable but powerful presence in day to day life.

These spirits easily translate to angels, while the almighty creator, too vast and remote to be understood, conforms to the notion of the one God. The embrace of Christianity and Islam, even today, is not necessarily to the exclusion of ancestral spirits, nor the essentials of witchcraft and sorcery. The precarious security of albino people in east and central Africa, whose body parts are sought after in traditional "medicine," is testimony to the fact that these superstitions are alive and well throughout Africa.

Dreams and Death in African Mythology: The History of Legends and Folk Stories about Dreams and Death across Africa examines the various stories that sought to explain death and dreams, from their origins to their evolution across different cultures. Along with pictures depicting important people, places, and events, you will learn about deaths and dreams in African mythology like never before.

The Creation Saga

The striking commonalities occurring in natural religions the world over arise from the fact that all peoples have been confronted with the same essential stimulus from the dawn of humanity. The sun and moon, the earth and sky, the elements, the eternal cycle, and the animals of nature all begged the same question to form the great and compound mystery. From this central mystery springs inexplicable systems of veneration and worship that, notwithstanding minor regional variations, possess common themes. The most famous polytheistic society in Africa, the ancient Egyptians, were dominated by Ra, the sun god, who merged with Amun-Ra to form the "Hidden One," the immutable and imponderable god of gods. The notion of a sun god is intuitive, for even the most primitive intelligence can ascertain the central nature of the sun in the cycle of life. Thus, the endowment of that phenomenon with divine properties would seem quite natural.

Africa comprises some 12 million square miles. It is over three times the size of Europe and accounts for 22% of the landmass of the world. A significant percentage of it is desert, including the great sand ocean of the Sahara Desert (covering some 3.5 million square miles), as well as the Namib, Kalahari, Nubian, Turkana, and Somali Deserts, which collectively add a similar area of uninhabited or sparsely inhabited regions to the whole. South of the Sahara, there lies the Sahel, a region of semi-desert, populated largely by pastoral nomads. The tropical regions stretch from the Atlantic coast of West Africa, the Bight of Benin, and through the basin of the Congo River. To the east and south lies the savanna belt, stretching south as far as the southern peninsula. One of the most significant, natural features of Africa is the Great Rift Valley, which commences in the Levant and reaches as far south as the Cape. However, its most recognizable features are the deep valleys and volcanoes of the central Rift, concurrent with modern Tanzania and Kenya, overlapping into the Great Lakes region and the continental divide.

Africa, as is common knowledge today, represents the cradle of humankind in which evolutionary threads of the human species separated from the apes. As the sciences of archaeology and anthropology continues to explore the earliest origins of mankind, fresh finds are still periodically unearthed, including the oldest hominin fossil found in Africa to date, which was unearthed in the deserts of Chad in 2001. The more recent movement and distribution of the human species across the face of Africa is somewhat easier to plot thanks, primarily, to the study of linguistics. To plot this in all of its detail, of course, would be impossible in a work of this size, but one can draw a broad delineation into six major language families. Afroasiatic languages are those spoken throughout North Africa, the Horn of Africa, and parts of the Sahel; the Austronesian languages are those spoken in Madagascar; the Indo-European languages, introduced by European colonists and often the *lingua franca* of large areas today, is usually in pidgin form; the Niger-Congo and Bantu languages are the most widely dispersed; and the Nilo-Saharan languages are spoken in places such as Sudan, Chad, and Mali.

As the Christian religion steadily marched toward domination of the Roman Empire, the symbolism became that of Christ. In Coptic and Ethiopian Christian imagery and iconography in particular, many Ancient Egyptian beliefs were repurposed for the sake of Christianity. This is evident in the enigmatic, 12th century Lalibela Churches of Eastern Ethiopia in which Pagan and Christian symbolism are both freely used at a time when one religion evolved to dominate another. The notion of Christ as the son of God merging with the great and almighty God, the one God, is uncannily similar to the merging of Ra with Amun-Ra to create a higher caste of divinity.

Africa was introduced to Christianity beginning with the Copts of Egypt, which influenced the establishment of Ethiopian Christianity, which manifests today in the Lalibela Churches. As is the case with Abrahamic faiths, their introduction into Pagan lands, those societies practicing shamanism or animism, occurred thanks to an overlap of beliefs and a fundamental compatibility between faiths. Today, Africa is dominated by the Christian faith, introduced in sub-Saharan Africa by European missionaries at the dawn of the imperial era. The cannons of Christianity proved compatible with the fundamentals of African belief structures. Barring the suppression of witchcraft, polygamy, and such devilish practices as drumming and dancing, the missionaries found it surprisingly easy to convert large numbers of black Africans. Historians point to the destruction of indigenous African society as a consequence of slavery and colonization, but many features of modern African Christianity contain strong, residual elements of traditional African religions.

The idea of God as the all-powerful, all-knowing creator of all things is a common enough theme in the African faith for Christian missionaries to make inroads. African folktales, particularly those seeking to explain natural phenomenon such and the sun, moon, and stars, invariably feature the intervention of a supreme being. However, prior to the introduction of Christianity and Islam, the belief in a monotheistic God was an alien notion. This is true insofar as the traditional African view of the supreme being was, and is, naturalistic, but there is always something present at the center of the universe that is singular, all-powerful, and immutable. Notwithstanding numerous, inevitable regional variations and different names, the similarities are often more striking than the differences.

In a nutshell, in the broader, universal sense, the African view of the supreme being is typically vague and ill-formed. The supreme being is almost always remote and dissociated from the more elemental, day-to-day human observances. It is a phenomenon that cannot be understood, and there are so few who still subscribe to animism to waste time trying. The world of ancestral spirits is far more present and immediate, and where a theocracy or priesthood exists to communicate and interpret the message of the supreme being, its work is arcane and beyond the knowledge of common men.

Onyangkopon of Ghana, *Ngai* or Kenya, *Mwari* of Zimbabwe, *Ruwa* of Tanzania, *Nkulungkulu* of South Africa, and a great many others all describe the existence of a supreme being. The presence of this supreme being, as with the Abrahamic God, helps account for the greater facts of creation lying beyond the tangible realities evident to the senses. Numerous names for, and definitions of, "God" have been chronicled by anthropologists over the years, but few if any definitive explanations have been offered as to the nature of that divinity. All that emerges is a head-scratching sense of neither knowing nor being particularly interested in whatever that element might be, but it does not typically intrude in the day to day lives of earthly men and women. The African supreme being is not the God of Islam and Christianity, demanding worship and veneration, but something utterly disinterested in the minutia of universal life; the responsibility of localized phenomenon belongs to a bewildering plethora of natural spirits.

Variations on the mythological character of the supreme being are not only regional but localized, with no two individuals inclined to agree when asked. Even in terms of creation myths, the idea that the supreme being created man alongside all the creatures of the earth, and indeed, the earth itself, is not universal. In the case of *Mulungu,* for example, the common Malawian name for the supreme being, legend tells of that being having asked from where all the beings and creatures wandering the earth have come. In other versions, the human species emerged from some spontaneous generation, while the animals are referred to as "*Mulungu's* people" in contradistinction from mankind.[1] Sometimes, the name of this supreme being is the same as the name for death. Not infrequently, death as a phenomenon is in some way connected to the work of a supreme being.

All of this leads to the matter of creation myths and stories which vary enormously from place to place and culture to culture. The creation myths and stories of Africa are so many and varied that we can only touch on a handful here. Most, in one way or another, are formed by the natural elements in existence around an individual people or interlinked group of peoples. The Nile, for example, obviously informed the ancient mythology of Egypt, and Mount Kilimanjaro influenced the creation myth of the *WaChagga* people of northeastern Tanzania.

The most widely distributed African language group by far is that of the Bantu. The story of the Bantus' dispersal is one of the most interesting sagas of African history. In a phenomenon known as the Bantu Migration, or as modern anthropology tends to prefer, the Bantu Expansion, the Bantu race radiated outward from its source to dominate much of Africa by way of incremental migration over hundreds of years. It would, perhaps, be fair to remark that most outsiders think of an "African" in terms of the typical "Negroid" or "Congoid" type, making up the vast preponderance of African population. These are the Bantu.

The Bantu originate in the region of the Niger Delta, bordering modern Nigeria and Cameroon. Sometime around 1,000 to 2,000 BCE, pressures on land and the later development of Iron Age technology prompted a steady, outward expansion. In its simplest terms, the movement spread

---

[1] Werner 1925:117

west and north but more vigorously east and south, moving first to occupy the central regions of the Congo Basin before crossing the continental divide and entering the conduit of the Great Rift Valley. This channeled the migrations north and south, eventually distributing the Bantu language across most of east-central Africa and vast swaths of the south. During the course of this advance, more ancient Neolithic races were displaced, absorbed, or assimilated. The only significant surviving example of this are the Bushmen or *San* of southern Africa who took refuge in the arid west of the subcontinent, where small pockets survive to this day.

It is estimated that over 1,000 distinct languages are spoken in Africa, with many thousands of associated dialects. The Congo, the largest African country, is home to over 325 distinct languages and many more dialects. Often, the original Bantu root was shaped by more ancient languages, and certainly, the modern languages of South Africa show the strong influence of the "click" style of the *San*. Then, there are languages such as Swahili, a Bantu language at its root, but influenced by Arabic and Indian vernacular introduced through international trade with the east coast of Africa. It was used as the Swahili lingua franca of trade in vast regions of the interior and dispersed the language as a common medium of communication, often as a second or third language, across most of Africa's east-central region.

This southward movement of the Bantu brought with it peculiar myths and legends associated with the ancient origins of the race, with many more gathered along the way. As a consequence, the mythology and folklore of Africa are dominated by Bantu tales and legends.

The regional concentration of cultural mythology tends to follow the density of population, and the most significant concentrations of the population have historically been in the tropical regions. Anthropologists have also noted that forest lifestyles and experiences tend to generate a particularly dense and vibrant mythology over time, associated with the far greater diversity of life pervading the forest. Forests also tend to limit physical vision, and in a world of deep recesses, dark shadows, and such a diversity of natural form, nature spirits proliferate with equal abandon. West and Central Africa are known for masks and fetishes. Deeper superstitions emerge among forest communities, and lives tend to be lived in constant intercommunication with unseen spirits of the forest.

Pre-colonized African society was a society in which the history was archived in the tradition of storytellers, and it is through this medium that the mythological foundation of any human society is established. Song and dance also occupy a place in the daily process of life, with specific songs and dances appropriate for each seasonal occupation and every social function in society. The recording of the oral tradition throughout Africa began around the turn of the 20th century and continues to this day, although the density and vivacity of the African oral tradition have faded to remnants under the influence of modernity.

The urge to understand the world and the machinations of nature has always been strong. In Africa, as is the case elsewhere, the creation myth is the central feature of social identity, and there are as many variations of it as there are individual societies and communities within the societies.

Perhaps the most quoted creation myths in encyclopedias of African mythology are those of the Yoruba, one of the principal language groups in modern Nigeria. From the Christianized south to the Islamized north, Nigeria offers up what is perhaps the broadest cultural and ethnic diversity in Africa, possessing a great depth of artistic and literary heritage. This story is told in many versions across Yorubaland, universally beginning with the actions of the Olodumare, or supreme being. Olodumare had two sons, the first, named Obatala, and the second, Odudwa. One day, Olodumare sent his sons to earth, giving them three things to carry: a bag, a hen, and a chameleon.

A common feature of every version of this story is that at the time, the earth was comprised of only water and no land. In more than one version of this tale, divinities accompany Olodumare's sons to Earth to prepare the land or create it on the water's surface. In others, it is discovered that the land is contained within a bag, first in the form of sand upon which a coconut palm is planted, and secondly, black soil within which the first crops are sown. Meanwhile, Obatala, the younger of the two brothers, discovers the coconut palm's ability to produce wine, which he drinks and then falls asleep. Oduduwa, the older brother, opens the bag and discovers the sand, which he spreads around the roots of the palm tree. He then releases the chameleon upon the surface of the sand. With the slow and careful gait of a chameleon, it determines that the beach is good and firm enough to bear weight. Next, the soil is spread out, and the hen is released. As hens are apt to do, she vigorously scratches and worries the soil, spreading it evenly, creating the land.

Soon enough, Oduduwa ventures to test the integrity of the land himself. As he does, Olodumare sends Prosperity down as a gift to him. Prosperity is typically depicted as female who brings with her seeds for cultivation, a bag of cowrie shells for trade, and three iron bars to be forged into knives, axes, and hoes. Thus, Oduduwa emerges as the first king of Ife, the first kingdom of Yoruba, while Obatala remains among the palms and becomes a drunkard.

Nigeria was one of the first regions in Africa to come under the influence of both Christianity and Islam. Christianity arrived at the coast with the first missionaries, while Islam was introduced from the north via trans-Saharan trade. As a consequence, Nigerian creation myths were modified under the influence of the Abrahamic tradition, as the character of traditional supreme beings were adapted and rationalized to suit the Christian and Islamic notions of God. In Nigeria, as in every British colony, individuals on trial or giving testimony in a court of law swore an oath to one of their traditional deities with their hand on a Christian Bible.

A variation of the Yoruba creation story follows the same essential theme, insofar as above there was only sky and below, only water. The sky was ruled by Olorun while his wife, the goddess, Olokun, ruled all that was below. This time, the hero is Obatala, a minor deity who requested and was granted permission from Olokun to create the earth for the use of living creatures. Obatala descended to the earth, bringing with him a gold chain upon which to climb down to earth, a snail's shell full of sand, a white hen, a black cat, and a palm nut, all of which was carried in a bag. The sand was spread, and the white hen released to scatter it about. Obatala called the place Ife and dug a hole to plant the palm nut. As he waited for a forest of palm trees to grow, he kept company with the black cat with whom he occupied himself, fashioning creatures out of clay. He became drunk on an intoxicating drink made from the palm, and the creatures he had made from clay, the people of the land, were imperfect, as the human race remains today. This angered Olokun who initiated a great flood.

In the savannah regions of the south is the *maShona* nation, a majority tribe in modern Zimbabwe. The term "maShona," it is perhaps worth noting, is not one that necessarily originated within the tribe itself. Today, it stands as an umbrella term for a dispersed group of individual clans and sub-groups, sharing a collective language and many common cultural traits, but who do not regard themselves as a unified people. The name was applied by the second major tribe of Zimbabwe, the *amaNdebele*, a close blood and ideological relative of the Zulu, and until the colonial period, the militarily dominant of the two. The maShona creation story, despite its central commonalities, varies in detail across a spectrum of clans and sub-clans. Nonetheless, the most commonly cited version tells a poignant love story between the earth and the heavens.

Mwari, the supreme being of maShona mythology, created Mwedzi, or the moon, in a deep pool of water. Characterized as male, Mwedzi implored Mwari to allow him to live on land. To relieve his loneliness, he was sent Hweva, the morning star, to be his wife. This, Mwari agreed to do, upon the understanding that Hweva would return to the firmament after two years. In those two years, Hweva conceived and gave birth to all the vegetation of the world. After two years, Mwedzi returned her to her home in the sky as promised, with profound reluctance. Soon, he was lonely again. This time, Mwari sent him the evening star, Morongo, sometimes Venekatsvimborume, under the same condition: that she must return in two years. Venekatsvimborume, too, conceived, giving birth to all the peace-loving birds, animals, and people of the world. However, when the time came for Morongo to return, Mwedzi would not allow it. Morongo immediately conceived again, this time giving birth to the violent predators: lions, crocodiles, poisonous snakes, and stinging creatures, like scorpions and wasps.

Mwedzi and Morongo's fate was for both of them to return to the sky, where they continue to reside to this day. The elements of this tale satisfy the question of earth and sky, the former temporal and the latter divine, along with the procreation of good and evil. It also touches on the importance and veneration of water and its divine power for good and evil. Water features prominently in local maShona mythology, an example of which is the initiation required of a novate spirit medium to live underwater for several years before emerging with the inner-vision necessary to communicate with the God and the spirits.

Another example of the curative power of water can be seen in a story explaining the difference between black and white. During the era of colonization, the curses of slavery and inequality were naturally seen in a racial context. Whites, with their overwhelming power of technology, wealth, and moral authority, were seen as blessed by God, while blacks, the subject of oppression, bondage, and misfortune, were seen as weak and cursed. It was told that a pool of cleanliness existed wherein Mwari ordered the people to wash. Those who were fortunate to find the pool full of water emerged white, while those arriving later to find the pool almost empty were only able to wash the palms of their hands and the soles of their feet.

The story of Unkulunkulu, the supreme being of the Zulu, is much simpler, and in some respects, more human, for Unkulunkulu derives from a human form. The Nguni, comprising the Xhosa, Zulu, Ndebele, and Swati sub-groups, are a Bantu people who originate in the eastern quarter of South Africa. The Nguni were widely scattered toward the end of the 18th and early 19th century by the advent of the Zulu wars. As a consequence, Nguni languages are spoken in regions as dispersed as Zimbabwe, Mozambique, and Malawi, with a similar dispersal of Nguni folklore and mythology.

Long ago, as the story goes, the earth existed only in darkness with nothing but a single seed representing life in its latent form. At some point, under ill-explained circumstances, the seed sank into the ground, and from it emerged a vast bed of reeds, known as "Uthanlga", or the source of all things. As time passed, a single reed transmuted into the form of a man, named Unkulunkulu, the "First Man" and creator of all things. In time, other reeds began to grow into men and women. Others grew cattle, fish, and wild animals. These Unkulunkulu plucked off their branches and set free on the land. He then created the mountains, rivers, valleys, wind, rain, sun, and moon. He taught the people to cultivate, cook, hunt, and make fire, and he named each and every creature of the earth.

Thus, Unkulunkulu was, indeed, the first man and the creator of all things, but he remained human. When all of this was complete, he sent out a chameleon to deliver the message to the people that they, like he, would be immortal. The chameleon went about this task very slowly, irritating Unkulunkulu who sent a speedier lizard in his wake to announce the presence of death. The lizard reached the village much sooner, and death has been among the people ever since. As the creator of all things, Unkulunkulu, remained immortal and divine.

In other versions of the tale, the lizard eavesdrops on chameleon's instructions, and out of envy, rushes ahead to deliver the opposite message. Another interesting aspect of this tale is that early Christians, who were often the first to commit the oral traditions of their converts to written archives, adapted the "messenger of eternal life" role of the chameleon, casting him as a symbol of Jesus Christ, without appreciating the nuance of the chameleon's position in Bantu mythology.

The notion of man having sprung from a plant is a common theme in Bantu mythology. The folklore of the Herero people of Namibia speaks of man springing forth from the "omumborombonga" tree. Other traditions suggest that man emerged from a cave. In societies such as the Nguni for whom cattle form a central social currency, man and cow often appear together. Another feature of Bantu mythology is the tendency for creation stories to dwell on the emergence of their own people without necessarily attempting to explain the creation of mankind as a whole. It was observed by early anthropologists that while the Zulu, Xhosa, and other allied groups coexisted for a period with the San, no effort was made to include the San in their tales of creation. It is possible they did not see the San as human in the same sense as themselves but created along with the wild animals, existing as a species different than man.

The Bakuba to the north in the Congolese rainforest is a dispersed tribe of the Congolese rainforest, a remnant of what had, at one time, been a powerful and dynastic kingdom dating back to the sixth century. The Bakuba creation myth tells of one great god, Mbombo, who was solely responsible for the creation of the universe. It is a curious tale filled with unexpected and ungodly imagery. Known sometimes as the "Great White Spirit," Mbombo ruled over a world comprised of only water in a universe of darkness in a theme strikingly similar to that of Unkulunkulu. That is, however, where the similarity ends. One day, after a particularly violent gastric upset, Mbombo vomited up the sun, moon, and stars. Suddenly there was light and warmth and from the heat of the sun, clouds rose from the water. As the level of the water dropped, so land began to appear.

Mbombo vomited again. This time, up came trees, animals, and people. In this way, by successive bouts of stomach upset, Mbombo eventually regurgitated all that is recognizable in the world today. The only product of all of this vomiting that was not benign in nature was lightning, which was so impulsive, unpredictable, and destructive that Mbombo eventually banished it from the earth to live in the sky, where it remains to this day. Lightning was, however, useful for the creation of fire. Exiled beyond the earth, the people were without fire, and Mbombo instructed them how to draw fire from trees. This periodically enraged lightning, causing it to strike the earth on occasion.

A depiction of Mbombo

There are numerous variations on the theme of God's creating man from clay, originating in every corner of the world. In Greek mythology, Prometheus fashioned men from clay, as did the Egyptian god, Khnum. A variation of the Yoruba creation story sees Obatala creating mankind from clay, and similar themes are found in cultures as widely dispersed as the Māori and Inca.

One such tale is told by the Shilluk people, described as a Luo Nilotic people of South Sudan, residing on both banks of the upper Nile. The supreme being of the Shilluk is Juok, who molded all the people of the world from clay. While he was involved in this work of creation, he wondered the world, finding clay in the land of the white man, and from this fashioned the white race. In Egypt, along the banks of the Nile, he encountered red mud from which he made the brown races. Lastly, when finding his way to the land of the Shilluk, he came upon the rich black earth in which all things grow, and from that, he created the black race.

As he sat with a lump of clay before him, Juok thought to himself, "I will give men long legs to run in the shallows while fishing, like the pink flamingos; I will give them long arms to swing a hoe the way a monkey swings a stick; I will give them mouths to eat millet and tongues to sing with; and I will give them eyes to see their food and ears to hear their songs."[2]

15

Other southern Sudanese variations tell of God baking his clay men and women in a bread oven, leaving them so long they burned, creating the black race. Trying again, anxious not to make the same mistake, he removed them from the oven early, and they were underdone, thus creating the white race. Trying for a third time, he succeeded; from this emerged the terracotta-colored people of the brown race which he considered perfect. They were, as a consequence, permitted to remain in the fertile regions of the Nile.

As was true with the River Nile, the prominent geography of a particular landscape often informed the mythology of the people residing upon it. As has frequently been the case throughout the history of mankind, mountains are endowed with peculiar significance. Wherever a great mountain is present, a deity invariably resides upon it. In Kenya, the Kikuyu deity, Ngai, occupies the summit of Mount Kenya, while Ruwa, the God of the Wachaga people of northeastern Tanzania, lives on Mount Kilimanjaro.

Table Mountain, known to the Khoisan as *Hoerikwaggo,* meaning "mountain in the sea," is the signature feature of the southernmost African city of Cape Town, and the home of Qamata, the supreme being of the Khoi. While busy creating dry land out the sea, a sea dragon, called Nkanyamba, tried to stop him. A great battle followed in which four great giants joined on Qamata's side. When the battle was over and the dragon defeated, the giants were turned to stone, forming the features of the mountain. The largest was given the name Umlindi Wemingizimu, or "Watcher of the South," and it became Qamata's home.

The Great Rift Valley is home to Africa's highest mountains and several major lakes, among them Lake Tanganyika, Lake Victoria, and Lake Malawi. Along the eastern shore of Lake Malawi resides a people known as the Yao, a branch of which are also coastal dwellers who have been in contact with Arabic traders for generations. They are, as a consequence, predominantly Muslim, but that does not preclude elements of ancient culture and faith in their folklore and mythology that remain evident today. It is their belief that in the earliest times, their traditional god, Mulungu, lived on the earth in a condition of peace and plenty. Death and cruelty were unknown until one day, a chameleon built a fish trap which he dropped into the river. The following morning, the trap was full of fish, which he ate before returning the trap to the water. Each day, his catch diminished until one day, all he found in the trap was a tiny man and woman. Having never seen such a thing, the chameleon took them to Mulungu who, after examining them, ordered that they be released on the earth to walk around.

Soon enough, the man and woman grew in stature, and the first thing they did was to strike a flint and start a fire which blazed through the forest. Animals were caught, killed, and cooked on the fire. Astonished at such cruelty and barbarity, the creatures of the earth fled. The chameleon went into a tree, followed by the spider who climbed so high he reached the sky. Mulungu begged to follow and was thrown down a thread of silk upon which he climbed to join the spider.

---

[2] Knappert, Jan. Pelizzoli, Francesca, ill. *Kings, Gods & Spirits from African mythology.* (Schocken Books, New York. 1986) p. 16.

Mulungu fled the earth to escape the brutality of mankind. There, he remained, adding his measure of blame to the maligned chameleon for bringing all of this about.

The chameleon, as we have heard, occupies a unique place in the mythology and superstitions of Africa, in particular among the Bantu. Even today, there are few native Africans who can abide being in the proximity of a chameleon. In many cases, the notion of the chameleon's otherworldly ability to change color and its curious mannerisms are tantamount to witchcraft, as is its role as the deliverer of evil spells. It also brings with it the message of death. A chameleon bite is reputed to have the effect of reversing good fortune, of turning a man into a woman, of inflicting a wound that cannot heal, or of causing madness. The lizard, who carries the message of death, is also despised, but not with quite the same irrational fear as the chameleon. The chameleon is found in the mythology and folklore of almost every African society. While it is almost always a malevolent character, neutral or helpful chameleons are not unheard of though rare. Chameleons can provoke infertility, madness, and melancholy, and when they die, their bones regrow in tiny replicas of themselves.

The Swahili people are perhaps one of the most famous and recognizable of the African races. They are a people of the Indian Ocean coast, stretching from the shores of Somalia to the island of Zanzibar. Their influence on the land and people of east and central Africa has been profound, evidenced by the geographic scope of the Swahili language spoken throughout Tanzania, Kenya, and Tanzania, and in large areas of Somalia, northern Mozambique, Rwanda, Burundi, and much of eastern Congo. Coastal dwellers, the Swahili traditionally acted as middlemen between the Arab and Indian traders of the coast and the vast resources of the interior. Through long exposure, the race is now predominantly Muslim, with considerable inter-breeding and the adoption of an Arab style of life, dress, and worship. The Swahili story of creation is the last one in this section, and predictably, it is an African adaption of ancient Semitic beliefs influencing both the bible and the Qur'an.

At first, there was only God, known as Mungu. God created a light. At first, it was only the dawn, but soon enough, there came the day, with light in all of its majestic spectrum, and He was pleased with the result. Then, in his omnipotence and all-knowing nature, he created everything that was, and all that would ever be. Every human being ever to reside upon the face of the earth was created at that moment, as was every thought, action, fortune, or misfortune until the end of time. First, came the souls of the prophets, the saints, the holy men, and the devout, who would exist only in the glory of Him, decreeing that their souls would reside forever in light. After this, God created the angels. Lastly, the common men and women of the world were created. Then, came the essential elements: the Canopy, the Throne, the Pen, the Book, the Trumpet, Paradise, and Hell.

The Canopy implies the shelter, vast and immutable, beneath which is the Throne. There, God resides in glory. The Pen, which bridges the earth and sky, writes the destiny of mankind, and the

Book is the receptacle within which all is written. This is done in order that all men will know and understand the law of God. The Trumpet is to announce the end of days and the time of judgment, opening a pathway for the soul of man either to Paradise or Hellfire.

On a somewhat less orthodox plane, beneath the Throne of God is a tree, known as the "Cedar of the End," the leaves of which are infinite in number, representing the lives of every individual living. When a leaf falls off the tree, it is swept up by an angel, known as Nduli Mtwaa-roho, or the "Reaper of all Souls," and taken to its representation on earth, which is then informed that his or her time has come. The sould is then taken, offering no respite or delay.

After creating the earth and all things on it, God created a cockerel of many colors who stands in heaven and heralds the day, prompting every cockerel on the face of the earth to do the same, inviting the faithful to wake and worship God. With the first crowing of the cockerel of many colors, the sun rises, the day dawns, and the world begins.

The Kingdoms of Africa

Much of Africa in the pre-colonial era existed under the dispersed rule of petty chieftainships and localized rulers. These were often only nominally loyal and usually linked by shared cultural and linguistic traits. It was this phenomenon that allowed early European colonists to avail themselves so easily of so much African land, to play one petty chieftain off another in an environment of mutual antagonism proved child's play, time and again. More difficult, however, was dealing with the few great kingdoms, the centralized monarchies ruling over large areas, and holding coherent and often militarized societies together. Egypt remains the most recognizable of the great African kingdoms, though for the sake of this narrative, we view the Egyptian culture as belonging more to Mediterranean civilizations. In sub-Saharan Africa, the iconic names are the Zulu, the Ashanti, the Kongo, and the Kings of Dahomey and Buganda.

By the advent of colonialism, many great African kingdoms had begun to fall into decline. The Portuguese, who arrived on the east coast of Africa toward the end of the 15th century, reported great cities of gold in the central interior, but by the mid-1880s and the "Scramble for Africa," all that remained were Great Zimbabwe's stone ruins. The empire of Ghana was founded in 700 CE. By 1067, Arab explorers from the coast of North Africa reported that the king of Ghana could field an army upwards of 200,000 men. By way of comparison, a year earlier, French Prince William of Normandy conquered England with an army of 7,000. The great Kingdom of Mali gathered strength with the founding of the Keita dynasty in 1235, which survived for two centuries. The Christian kings of Aksum followed the decline of the Kingdom of Kush, the former in Ethiopia and the latter in South Sudan. When the Portuguese reached the Swahili coast, they encountered city-states scattered along the Indian Ocean seaboard and a strong, regional, commercial center in Zanzibar. Further south, toward the end of the 18th century, the powerful Zulu warrior, King Shaka, emerged to unite the disparate tribes of the Nguni into one of the greatest warrior empires in African history.

A European depiction of Shaka

Perhaps one of the most sophisticated and accomplished kingdoms in Africa was the Buganda, which was still viable and in existence when the territory of Uganda was declared a British protectorate. The Buganda kings were able to trace their common origins to a man named Kintu, perhaps originating in South Sudan, who invaded from the north. Kintu was certainly a certainly an authentic historical figure, but he has also become the subject of mythological tales that have since taken on aspects of creation stories. Certainly, the encyclopedia's description of Kintu is as a mythological figure who appears in legends from Buganda in a creation myth.

In the beginning, Kintu arrived in Uganda as something of a wandering spirit, unaccompanied by an army and bringing with him the essentials of millet grain, cattle, and bananas, all gifts given to him by the sky god, Mugulu. Mugulu also sent his eldest daughter, Nambi, and her unnamed, younger sister down from the sky. In some versions of this story, it is Mugulu's sons who come to earth in the company of their sister, Nambi, but in each case, they encounter Kintu and engage him in conversion. Nambi is impressed with Kintu and decides that she would like to marry him. She is, however, cautioned by her father and siblings that Kintu might not be all that he seems. Indeed, it was not really possible to determine if he was even human. This leads to the requirement that Kintu prove his humanity, which he does through a series of five trials.

These trials adopt a herculean flavor when he is required to complete a mammoth meal, cut stone with a copper axe, fill a pot with dew, and select a particular cow from a herd of thousands. Each task he completes, in part, thanks to the intervention of some kindly but mystical creature and, in part, because of his resource and ingenuity. Kintu is duly married to Nambi and inherits the kingdom of the earth.

Another powerful, dynastic kingdom of Uganda was the Bunyoro, which existed in the east of Uganda from the 13th to the 19th century. As is the case with Kintu, the saga of the first man is often the same as that of the first king, and often that of the first or supreme god. The Bunyoro origin story is striking similar to that of Buganda but with reversed gender roles.

In the early times, there was only the heavens and the underworld. Heaven was the home of the gods while the underworld was populated by outcasts from heaven who took on strange forms. One day, Isaza, son of Supreme God Ruhanga, grew curious of life in the underworld and decided to visit. There, he was fascinated by the curious lives and customs of the outcasts, and he fell in love with and married an outcast princess.

The story continues, for Isaza cannot now return to the sky, so he settles in the underworld and begins a family. The princess bears him a son by the name of Isimbwa, who finds his way back to the land of the gods. One day, after many years, he returns to the earth where he discovers an illegitimate commoner by the name of Bukubu and gains power over the kingdom of his father. Bukubu was told by a diviner that his eldest daughter would give birth to a challenger. To prevent this, the girl has her breasts and one eye removed to make her unattractive, and she is locked away in a safe place. Isimbwa, however, gains access to the place and copulates with the girl, who soon afterward, produces a baby boy, called Ndahura. When he learns of this, Bukubu orders the child to be killed, and he is thrown into a river. He somehow survives and one day assassinates Bukubu and takes his place on the royal stool. So it was that Ndahuru became king and ruler of the Kingdom of the Bunyoro, expanding the empire to cover much of modern Uganda, western Kenya, Rwanda, Burundi, parts of northern Tanzania, and eastern Congo. He is, as a consequence, an authentic historical figure, merging into a mythological hero with divine aspects.

Mention is made in the above story of a royal stool, which brings us to our final story of the kings and kingdoms of Africa. The stool as an article of furniture and cultural accoutrement is extremely important throughout the west and equatorial Africa, denoting authority from the humblest of homesteads to the highest sovereignty of a nation. The spirit of a man is said to reside in his stool, and from village councils to national legislatures, each member brought his own stool. It is difficult, then, to understate the significance of this humble article of furniture.

One of the greatest of the West African kingdoms was the Ashanti, which came into direct conflict with Britain when the British Empire sought to gain control of the gold reserves of what was then known as the Gold Coast. This was one of the epic sagas of African resistance to colonization, and much of the fighting was focused on retaining and capturing the Golden Stool.

Sika Da Kofi, or the "Golden Stool Born on Friday," was the symbol of Ashanti sovereignty, and it was guarded and protected through the succession of Ashanti wars in much the same as the Roman legion fought for its *aquila*. When the Golden Stool was eventually surrendered by the Ashanti, it marked the effective end of resistance.

The significance of the Golden Stool is fortified by an origin story containing mythic elements. According to legend, the stool was summoned to earth on a Friday by Okomfo Anokye, the chief priest of the land, who brought it to rest at the feet of Osei Tutu, proclaiming his right to rule. Anokye declared the stool to contain the spirit of a new kingdom, and he decreed that all lesser stools be destroyed. The genius of this proclamation lay in cementing military and secular elements of the rise of the Ashanti with spiritual symbolism and divine endorsement. Osei Tutu reigned from 1675-1680 and was rather like Kintu and Ndahura, a synthesis of mortal and divine, and the factual and mythological.

Death and the Dead

From the point of view of ethnographic and anthropological study, Africa tends to be divided into two broad delineations – those being Saharan and sub-Saharan Africa. North Africa has historically been placed within the orbit of Mediterranean history, and later Middle Eastern history. Sub-Saharan Africa stands as a region separate, isolated from Europe and the Mediterranean by the great sand sea that is the Sahara Desert. As a consequence, sub-Saharan Africa was also insulated from the vast sweep of Islam, and certainly from Christianity which did not begin to make any serious inroads until the advent of the colonial period. Islam, of course, gained a foothold on the east coast of Africa thanks to the ancient trade links between the Swahili coast and the Arabian Peninsula, but its influence in the interior remained limited. As a consequence, sub-Saharan Africa remained largely isolated from the great social and religious permutations of the post-Christian era, developing only according to the internal movements and migrations that have shaped modern Africa.

About 7,000 years ago, the ancestors of the Khoisan of South Africa began their slow ambulation south, followed five millennia later by the Bantu, who displaced the San as they steadily advanced to occupy the central region and most of the southern subcontinent. This process of migration, which, of course, contained many more facets that just those two described above, facilitated a wide cross-pollination of ideas and mythologies, one borrowing from another as the generations passed. In the broad absence of a written language, oral tradition played a key role in the spread of knowledge and the archiving of history across the African continent. The tradition of African storytelling developed over thousands of years, perpetuated tradition and history in a vast archive of folktales and parables, only a fraction of which have ever found their way into archived history.

Until the advent of colonization, the only sub-Saharan African society with indigenous traditions of written language were those directly impacted by outside religion. Ethiopia, for example, was the first sub-Saharan kingdom to adopt Christianity, and there a domestic syllabary system was developed to write Amharic. The Swahili-speaking peoples of the African coast also used a system of written language but based on Arabic text, although this was highly specialized and did not extend very far into the interior. Thus, oral tradition and the tradition of storytelling were vital not only in the exchange of information and the archiving of tribal memory but also in defining the individual cultural identity of distinct groups, who, although identifying separately, nonetheless often shared a broad language root.

Perhaps one of the least studied and most underappreciated African nation is that of the San, or the Bushmen, an ancient race of hunter-gatherers who lived, and in many instances still live in very close commerce with nature. Perhaps the most striking aspect of San society and culture is the vast and widely dispersed tableau of parietal art, displaying not only a unique style but also great technical accomplishment. The objective of San cave art was religious-spiritual, insofar as depictions of animals not only presaged a successful hunt, but it was also simply narrative, created to record the signature events of day-to-day life. Examples, some very minor, and some forming vast frescos, can be found all over southern Africa, indicating the extent to which the San ranged the region before the arrival of the Bantu. There are examples of San rock art depicting people of taller stature and broader build, indicating the arrival among the San of the more robust and adaptable Bantu. Yet others depict wagons, horses and riders, marking the moment that the white man appeared on the ancient landscape of Southern Africa.

The first attempt to record Bushman mythology and folklore was complicated considerably by the curious language of the San which comprises a vocabulary of click consonants that are not shared by any other African language, and which even today is used and borrowed by very few non-San. Several dialects, often spoken by just a few families, have in time become extinct, and it is fortunate that so much work in recording Bushman oral history was done before the worst ravages of modernity. For this, we mainly thank the German linguist Wilhelm Bleek and his English sister-in-law Lucy Catherine Lloyd, who, besides a great deal more work, together produced the book *Specimens of Bushman Folklore*, first published in 1911. This important, if rather inaccessible volume, recorded only eighty-seven legends, myths and other traditional stories of the ǀXam Bushmen, interpreted from a language that is now extinct.

The manner in which *Specimens of Bushman Folklore* is written is interesting insofar as it records verbatim the interpretation of each individual story, echoing the curious syntax of the San "click" language. For example, one reads, "The children are those who approached gently to lift the Sun-armpit, while the Sun-armpit lay sleeping. The Children felt that their mother was the one who spoke; therefore, the children went to the Sun; while the sun shone, at the place where the sun lay, sleeping lay."[3] This story, entitled "The Children Are Sent to Throw the Sleeping Sun Into the Sky," describes the curious Bushman legend of the Sun which is told widely and with many variations. The reason that the children were given this task differs broadly in the telling, from the desire of an old woman to dry her wild rice to dissatisfaction with the selfish use of light by the Sun himself.

"The children came, the children went; the old woman said: *'You must go to sit down, while Ye wait for him.'* Therefore, the children went to sit down, while the children waited for him; he lay down, he lifted his elbow, his armpit shone upon the ground, as he lay. Therefore, the children threw him into the sky while they felt that the old woman had spoken to them."[4]

Similarly, there is a story about the little girl who threw glowing ashes into the sky to create the Milky Way. She is usually described as being of the "Old Race," and as the story goes, she arose one night in a somnambulatory state, and burying her hands in the hot ashes of the fire, she was burned and flung them skyward in pain.

"The wood ashes which are here, they must altogether become the Milky Way. They must white lie along in the sky, that the stars may stand outside the Milky Way, while the Milky Way is the Milky Way, while it used to be wood ashes."

The Bushmen lived in very close proximity to nature. They were a nomadic hunter-gatherer people who forswore property and lived entirely in harmony with nature. No animals were domesticated and no plants adapted for cultivation. As a consequence, they were uniquely close to nature, more conscious of its facets, and almost the entirety of their social culture was written, and spoken in the language of nature. Many of the Bushman tales have a fireside flavor about them and they are often extremely abstract and enigmatic. A close cultural relative of the San are those traditionally referred to as the "Hottentot," an onomatopoeic name given to the Khoi by the Dutch because of the curiosity of their language. The original Khoisan of the Cape entered practical extinction soon after the arrival of the white man, through extermination, assimilation and interbreeding, although the gene pool, albeit diluted, remained strong. Indeed, many of the more colorful folktales of earlier times transitioned, and entered the folklore of the frontier Dutch, taking on the character of their own observation of nature and the land around them. Many of the creation stories traceable to the San have similar versions told in more orthodox terms by Dutch and Coloured oral archivists.

The Zulu origin of the death story involved two messengers, the chameleon and the lizard, the former the agent of immortality and the latter the agent of death. A similar theme can be found in the Bushman tale of the moon, the hare and death. Moon once instructed Hare to go to the land of men and deliver to them the message that as the moon died and was resurrected, so would

---

[3] Bleek, W.H.I and Lloyd, L.C. *Specimens of Bushman Folklore.* (George Allen & Company, London, 1911) p45
[4] Ibid.

mankind. Somehow this message was perverted into a message of death, and this happens by numerous means, with the single commonality of Hare reporting back to Moon the erroneous nature of the message. So enraged was Moon that she picked up a stick and hurled it at Hare, splitting his lip, which is why Hare has had a split lip ever since. Moreover, Hare ran away and still runs to this day. Some versions claim that Hare leapt up, and with his powerful back claws, scratched the face of Moon, leaving the scars that can still be seen by the light of a full moon.

In another version of the same story, there are two messengers, Hare and an insect. The insect, probably a mantis, was the one charged by Moon with delivering the message of resurrection, but beguiled and corrupted by Hare, a message of death was delivered instead.

Another origin of the death tale told by the *Kung* clan of the San, who are still to be found in the Etosha region of Namibia, involved a character frequently found in Bushman mythology, Heiseb, the hero-magician. One day, Heiseb and his wife and infant son were foraging for food and came upon a bush laden with delicious berries. The little boy ran toward the bush and began shoveling berries into his mouth. Heiseb scolded him for his greed, at which the boy collapsed and pretended to be dead. Believing that he *was* dead, Heiseb dug a grave and buried him. However, later, when the boy decided he was bored with the game and came out of the grave, he was met by his mother, who was overjoyed. Heiseb, however, would not believe it, and decided that the dead should remain dead. He killed his son, therefore, and returned him to the grave. Only death thereafter resided in that place, and the Bushmen believe that all men die for that reason.

A strikingly similar story is told among the Maasai, thousands of miles to the north on the equator. The Maasai exist within the Bantu-speaking world, but they are a Nilotic people of distinct appearance, and in a land of strangers, and inferior strangers at that, they have a rather proud and aloof nature. The traditional ranges of the Maasai overlap Kenya and Tanzania, a region of strong Bantu influence, where a great many distinct languages and dialects are spoken, and Maasai mythology, as a consequence, is inescapably influenced by the world of the Bantu.

In times of old, the supreme god, known to the Maasai by the name of Naiteru-kop, instructed a man called Le-eyo that if a child should die for any reason, the body was to be thrown away and certain words chanted in ritual. These were – "Man die and come back again; moon die and remain away."

Soon afterwards, a child did indeed die, but it was not one of Le-eyo's own children, so when he threw the body away, the words he sang were – "Man die and remain away; moon die and return."

Then, however, sometime later, one of his children did die, and throwing the body away, he chanted this – "Man die and return; moon die and remain away."

The exasperated Naiteru-kop declared that it was no use trying again, and his first utterance would stand, and so it was that the moon was permitted to resurrect while man was condemned to death.

While we have heard already of the Zulu tale of the lizard and the chameleon, and the message of death, among the Akamba, a Bantu tribe of modern-day Kenya, a similar story is told involving the chameleon and the thrush. This is a rather mysterious story in which God, or the Supreme Being, gathered before him the chameleon, the thrush and the frog. To all three, he gave the instruction to go forth and discover people who have died and been resurrected. The frog, however, while attending the summons, appears to play no role thereafter in the narrative, and he leaves the stage to the thrush and the chameleon. Chameleon was in those days a proud and commanding animal, of high rank in the hierarchy of God's creatures, and it was he who led the way. When he came upon a group of human corpses, he whispered to them, *"Niwe Niwe Niwe."*

Thrush asked why, to which chameleon replied that he was calling them to resurrect.

"The dead are dead, and they remain dead," retorted Thrush, always a little jealous of Chameleon. The human dead would not respond to Chameleon's message of eternal life but listened instead to Thrush, and so they remained dead. Disconsolately, Chameleon returned to the deity to report this turn of events, after which, Thrush was summoned and ordered to explain himself. Thrush, however, with his beguiling song, convinced the deity that chameleon was a fool who bungled the message, forcing Thrush to interrupt. Chameleon protested, but was not believed, and was demoted in the estimation of the deity, while Thrush was given the honorable job of awakening men from their slumber which he does to this day.

A similar story is told in Togo, West Africa, this time involving a frog and a dog. This time too the sequence is somewhat reversed insofar as the dog was given the task by men to approach God with a request that upon their death they wished to be resurrected. Thus instructed, the dog set off, but behind him followed a frog intending to inform God that men did *not* desire resurrection. Why he wished to do this is nowhere explained, for the frog is not typically a malicious creature in African folklore, but nonetheless, that was his intention.

Dog, in the meanwhile, feeling hungry, smelt something delicious, and he was irresistibly diverted to the hut of a man boiling magic herbs. Thinking that he was cooking food, the dog sat down to wait for his share. He noticed Frog passing as he sat, but it did not concern him. Frog, of course, found his way to the deity soon afterwards, and gave the message, purportedly from men, requesting that when death found them, that they would not like to return to life. Accepting this curious request, the deity dismissed Frog, and off he hopped.

Soon afterwards, however, Dog appeared before the deity and submitted his request, also on behalf of men, that upon their deaths they *would* like to return to life. This, of course, was puzzling, and after thinking about it for some time, the deity determined that he would accept the first message, and thus when men die, their deaths are permanent.

A version of the death story is told by the Ashanti of Ghana with the main characters a sheep and a goat. In the old times, God lived among men in an age of happiness and plenty. Men were given all that they asked for and were refused nothing. One day, however, God was banished from the earth by a group of women pounding grain in mortars. In some versions, he was sent on his way with a thorough beating with pestles. For a long time thereafter, at his place in the sky, he nurtured a grievance, but in time he was mollified, and he sent a goat to earth with a kindly message. That message was a warning of a thing known as death that would likely come and harm them. Even if it did, however, death need not be permanent, and men would enjoy communion with God in heaven. The goat, however, was distracted by a succulent bush which he paused to nibble on.

Noticing this, God gave the same message to a sheep. The sheep, however, muddle-headed and rather simple, confused the message and informed the men that God had decreed that when they died, they would never return. This melancholy message was accepted, and when finally goat arrived with his message of immortality, the men would not believe him.

The Nandi of Kenya, in the meanwhile, tell yet another version of the origin of death story, this time concerning the moon and a dog. In this simple tale, a dog entered the village of men and demanded milk and beer, adding that if he was given what he asked for, men would resurrect three days after dying, as the moon did. The humans agreed, but gave the dog his milk and beer in a bowl on the ground, and not as they themselves took it. He drank what was given to him, but told them upon his leaving that the moon would die and rise again, but men would remain dead for eternity.

Our final death story is a curious tale that concerns a journey to the Land of the Dead, told in numerous versions all over West Africa. A couple, as yet childless, and married for just a short time, decided one day to travel to the village of the wife's family to visit her parents. They set off early in the morning, walking through the cool forest until they came to the banks of a wide and shallow river. There the man was surprised to see a skull resting on the path, and even more surprised when the skull spoke, pleading to be carried across the river. While the man was reluctant, his wife, somewhat incautiously, persuaded him to help, and so he fetched up the skull in his hand and stepped into the water. On the far side, however, when he tried to set the skull down, it bit his finger, and in a threatening tone, ordered that he be placed on the man's shoulder. Feeling a sense of dread, the man complied, and when told by the skull to continue walking, the couple did.

Before long they found themselves in an unfamiliar part of the forest, and as evening settled, they saw that they were surrounded by whispering, taunting bats, thanking the skull for bringing them fresh meat. Entering a ghostly village, the skull asked to be set down before ordering the terrified couple to go into the forest to gather firewood for the fire that would be used to roast them.

However, while about this task, the man almost upset a delicate spider's web, and as he approached, he was amazed to hear the spider plead with him to stop. After hearing the woeful tale, the spider summoned a tiny antelope, and upon its back, he led the couple back to the village of ghosts. Once there, and as the evil spirits, no longer in the form of bats, lingered waiting for their meal, the spider spun a web around the village, trapping the spirits within it. The man and woman were freed from their dreaded fate, and from that day on, no spiderweb was ever disturbed in their home.

This story is, of course, something of a cautionary tale derived from an era when the forest was a vast and forbidding entity, littered with evil spirits and threatening entities, its human population small and dispersed. The land of the dead is usually subterranean, and villages of the dead often tend to be purgatorial, and populated less by the host of ancestral spirits, who are on the whole benign and helpful, than the more mysterious less definable spirits of nature.

The land of the dead, or the village of the dead, both form a common theme in the mythology of west and central Africa, and not always are they places of dread and trepidation. Another curious tale of the land of the dead, commonly told in West Africa, involves the wounding of a porcupine. One night, a young man was given a spear by a village elder and instructed to keep an eye on the corn patch. At dusk, he spied a porcupine, and throwing the spear, he hit the porcupine which fled with the spear embedded in its side. The village headman, when he heard, was irritated at the loss of his spear, and he ordered the youth to follow the porcupine and find it.

Doing as he was told, the young man crawled into the porcupine's hole and was surprised when it widened into a long tunnel several miles in length. Eventually, the tunnel led to a lush and beautiful land where the boy was greeted by his father who had been dead for many years. When hearing the tale of the spear and porcupine, the father revealed to his living son that the porcupine was his dead mother who sometimes roamed the land of the living in animal form. Finding his mother seated in a hut with the spear leaning against the wall, the son was heartsore to learn that he had wounded his own mother. From the fire, however, she conjured a fat ram, which she gave to the boy, and a small vial of snuff. He sniffed a pinch of the snuff, as he was instructed, and he was impressed with the pleasant sensation. The substance, his mother told him, was tobacco, and with that, she gave him a handful of seeds, and by some magic, he found himself back in the maize field with the ram and the spear. The village elder gratefully accepted the return of the spear, and he too tried the snuff and agreed it was excellent. The young man planted the seeds and cultivated the tobacco, endowing the word with pleasure and himself with wealth.

Dreams, Spirits, and Monsters

Dreams occupy an important space in the mythology and folklore of every continent and every race, and in almost every case, dreams represent a medium of communication and a parallel experience alongside or within the spirit world. Dreams exist as an important thread in the Australian Aboriginal creation narrative, and many ancient cultures, among them the Egyptians, left textual reference to the science of dream interpretation. The Babylonians and Assyrians believed that dreams were either good or evil, the former sent by the gods and the latter by demons. Indeed, in an ancient text known as the *Iskar Zaqiqu,* various dream scenarios are recorded along with predictions and prognostications on what might occur if an individual dreams such a dream. Both the Indians and Chinese believed in the external journey of the soul during Dreamtime, while Morpheus, the Greek god of dreams, sent prophecies and warnings through the agency of dreams to those who slept in shrines and temples.

In Africa, dreaming and dreams are of no less significance and are almost universally regarded as the arena of communication with the ancestors. Dreams are comprehensible only to those with the gifts to read and understand them. South African spiritual healers and mystics, known generally as "Sangoma," place a great deal of emphasis on the interpretation of dreams. Those, for example, who dream of snakes, or water, are gifted with spiritual insight. Common dreams of nakedness are seen as a harbinger of an evil spell, or that the dreamer is a victim of witchcraft, as is also true in dreaming of food or eating. Dreaming of a wedding is a warning of death, and when dreaming of death, or of a dead person, it is an indication of an attempt from the other side to make contact.

A commonality across Africa, however, and in most corners of the world, is that dreaming is the journey of the spirit. In each person, there exists, as a life force, a soul, or a shard of the great, universal spirit which is released to freely wander during Dreamtime. In the beginning, say the Yoruba, there was only the divine spirit of Orisha and his slave Eshu. Eshu chafed and rebelled against his lot in life, and sought to kill Orisha. One day he rolled a huge boulder over a cliff that landed on Orisha's house, splintering it into an infinite number of pieces. However, since he was divine, Orisha's spirit could not be killed, but instead, it was spread through the wreckage of his hut into every person, every creature, every tree and every element.

Africa was, as in many places it remains, a land where witchcraft and sorcery exist as a daily fact of life. Any and every misfortune, illness or reversal is explainable as a curse, or an act of witchcraft. Witches and sorcerers are to be found everywhere, and nothing is as it seems, for shapeshifters abound, and witches can ride hyenas, or even transform into a hyena, or a snake, indeed, as our next story confirms.

Two brothers once argued over the powers of a python, and how each would respond if they should come upon one. The younger of the two claimed that if he encountered a python, he would simply draw his knife and kill it. At this, the other laughed, quite sure that if his younger brother did stumble across a python, he would die of fright. The two parted company, and that night, as the younger brother slept in his hut, a python entered the open doorway and began to devour him. The young man awoke and was astonished to apprehend half of his body already swallowed. However, as he said that he would, he drew his knife and cut the python's jaw, by which means he was able to free himself. The wounded python fled.

The next morning, the man hurried to the hut of his brother to tell him the tale, and after knocking on the door, and receiving no answer, he allowed himself in. There, on his sleeping mat, lay his brother, bleeding, and close to death from a terrible wound to his mouth.

This story is told in numerous versions and forms throughout West Africa and is a part parable and part cautionary tale. The shapeshifter theme, however, is a common one throughout Africa, and indeed, in many other parts of the world. European colonists and settlers were often confronted with a barrier of communication when dealing with the absolute belief of common people in their superstitions. The memoirs of early medical missionaries to Africa are filled with frustrated stories of their war against superstition and witchcraft as they tried to explain modern hygiene and disease.

In 1987, the Supreme Court of South Africa was confronted with a curious incident of murder. The case involved a young Xhosa man by the name of Naletzane Netshiavha who stood accused of killing a man with an axe. The story told by the accused in his own defense was simply this: late one night he was awoken by a persistent scratching at his door, and fetching up an axe, he went to investigate. To his horror and astonishment, he saw what he identified as an enormous bat hanging from the rafters of his room. He instinctively swung his axe and struck the creature, cutting a deep wound into its body, after which he fled. Having alerted others in the village, a group of armed men returned, and there, in the moonlight, they could clearly see the creature dragging its bleeding form across the courtyard. It was promptly attacked and beaten to death, and then, as every witness later testified, the body began slowly to take on the form of a child which grew quickly into an adult. The body was that of a certain Jim Nephalana, a notorious, self-confessed wizard with powers to change himself into any form he chose.

Presented with this story, a white Supreme Court Magistrate, after giving it due consideration, was forced to consider only the verifiable facts, and since no one, not even the accused, denied that he had killed the creature, he was by his own admission culpable. The hammer thus came down on a verdict of guilty.

It would probably be worth noting that the creature thus described was a *tokoloshe*, an adaptable umbrella term for an evil spirit or a mischievous sprite, usually thought of as a goblin-like creature. *Tokoloshe* can range from an impish scoundrel to a blood-soaked, malevolent killer. Tokoloshe are ubiquitous in South African folklore and mythology, and very much alive and well in the consciousness of a majority of the modern population.

Shapeshifters, of course, can also be animals that take on human form, and the examples of this are many. The *Impundulu*, is a legendary bird commonly found in Zulu and Xhosa mythology, also known as the lightning bird, who guards the dens of witches and wizards, and frequently assumes human form. The Impundulu not infrequently displays vampire tendencies, although its eggs are known to possess healing properties.

Inkanyamba is an eel of monstrous size that populates Zulu and Xhosa legend, with powers to control the weather, and found in numerous parables and cautionary tales. The *Grootslang* is another South African monster and an example of the crossover of native folklore to Dutch.

The Dutch, it might perhaps be worth noting, made landfall in South Africa in 1652, so by the later 18th and 19th centuries, a deeply founded white culture existed on the landscape with deep layers of its own folklore and mythology – a synthesis of both North European and African.

The *Grootslang* was a snake so enormous that the gods decided it must be divided into two, one half snake and the other elephant. Some survived unchanged, and today the *Grootslang* is known to live in a cave known as the "Wonder Hole" in the Richtersveld region of South Africa. Because the beast was so sub-divided, it is very rare, for only a few escaped being split in this way. The Wonder Hole is reputed to be filled with diamonds, but so well guarded by the *Grootslang* that no one dares investigate.

A commonly described mythological monster is the *Kongamato*, so named in parts of northern Angola, western Zambia and southern Congo. Variations of it, however, are also described throughout equatorial and West Africa. The *Kongamato* is a huge, winged reptile, something akin to a *pterosaur*, that lives in rivers, swamps and other fetid and unhealthy places. Somewhat like the Bigfoot legends of North America, sightings of the *Kongamato* are frequent, and in fact, in 1932, the British explorer Frank Welland recorded and described an encounter with the creature. Kongamato features in early Hollywood depictions of Africa; for example, in the early renditions of Tarzan.

The Ewe people of Ghana and Togo tell the story of a vampire-like creature, the *Adze*, that exists as a butterfly, and sometimes a firefly, approaching the unwary, upon which it suddenly is turned into an ogre-like human that drains a victim's blood and steals their organs. It is typically invulnerable, and sometimes takes the form of a mosquito, sucking blood and spreading disease. It has been suggested that this represents an early appreciation of the cause and effect of malaria, although there is a strong front of skepticism against this. The word "malaria" is derived from the Italian *"mal aria,"* meaning bad air, and it was not until the late 19th century that any correlation between the bite of a mosquito and the onset of malaria was made.

Gods of nature form a common thread throughout African mythology, and once again, the regions most thickly populated by such gods and deities are the rain forests of west and central Africa. It is rare, however, to encounter a nature god of African mythology that clashed so directly with the modern march of progress than the river god of the Tonga people of the Zambezi Valley. The Tonga were, and in places still are a river people populating both banks of the Zambezi River, straddling the nations of Zimbabwe and Zambia.

As with all races living in such close association with a major natural feature such as a mountain, a lake or a river, the mythology of the Tonga is deeply intertwined with the Zambezi River, and in particular the Zambezi River God Nyami Nyami. Nyami Nyami has become popularized by the modern tourist industry centered around the Victoria Falls, and frequently found in local folk art, printed T-shirts and similar iconography. He is typically portrayed in the form of a fish-headed snake, alluding, of course, to the snake-like qualities of the river, and the fish that it contains.

In the late 1950s, however, as Southern and Northern Rhodesia were developing as British colonies, the Zambezi Valley was a remote and isolated place, and the Tonga a little known, barely contacted and highly traditional people. It was in that year that the colonial authorities made the decision to dam the Zambezi River at the Kariba Gorge, which would necessitate the relocation of the river-dwelling Tonga to higher land. The tribal elders resisted, however, assuring their people that Nyami Nyami would never allow the river to be stopped or blocked. Despite this, planning went ahead, and in 1957, with work on the construction of Kariba Dam well underway, the Zambezi River flooded with record water levels, destroying and compromising much of the construction underway downstream. This offered temporary vindication for those predicting the wrath of the river god, and it certainly gave everyone food for thought, but it did not ultimately halt the construction of the dam, and nor the relocation of the Tonga away from the rising waters.

Another river god story that originates in the region of the Lower Zambezi, and elsewhere along the east African coast of Mozambique, is the legend of *Chipfalamfula*, another river god that likewise takes the form of giant fish. *Chipfalamfula* is typically described as a great fish, but also sometimes a snake, or eel-like creature, usually with a large mouth. *Chipfalamfula* possesses the power to control the physical properties of a river, including its propensity to flood during the monsoon and dry up during a drought. Of generally kindly disposition, *Chipfalamfula* is known to rescue those drowning in his waters, and he is particularly fond and protective of children. Even to this day, a large fish caught out of any river is referred to as *Chipfalamfula*.

There are many recorded tales of *Chipfalamfula*, but the most common concerns Chief Makenyi, whose youngest wife bore him two beautiful daughters, the eldest of whom was named Chichinguane. The chief's fondness for his youngest wife and her two delightful daughters stirred up considerable envy among the other, less favored wives and offspring, and it was Chichinguane in particular who found herself often the target of spite. One day, as was a common chore, the girls of the village went down to the river to collect the clay that was used for plastering the huts. The older girls forced Chichinguane to climb down into the clay pit and fill the baskets, but when the task was complete, they left without helping her out. The pit was situated adjacent to the river, and so, when a sudden rainstorm came, and the river water began to flood in, and it seemed that the unfortunate child would drown.

Suddenly, however, *Chipfalamfula* appeared, his great mouth agape. Chichinguane was invited to enter into his mouth, and she did. Inside the belly of the fish, she found a strange world of contented people, living their lives in peace and happiness, and there Chichinguane remained for many days. One day, however, not long afterwards, the girls of the village returned to the same spot on the river, this time to collect water. Among them was Chichinguane's little sister who was unable to lift her earthenware water pot onto her head once it was full. The other girls, of course, abandoned her, but to her surprise, she saw her sister Chichinguane walking out of the water and onto dry land. Chief Makenyi, of course, and the mother of the girls had both assumed that Chichinguane had drowned. After helping to lift her sister's burden, Chichinguane walked with her a short distance towards the village before returning to the river.

For a few days the sisters met on banks of the river, and each time Chichinguane helped lift the full water pot onto her sister's head. One day, however, the child's mother noticed that she was unable to lift a full pot of water, and she asked then how was she able to bring water back from the river. When it was explained to her how Chichinguane appeared from the water each morning to help, both mother and daughter hurried to the river, and there, true enough, Chichinguane was waiting.

Chichinguane, however, would be neither touched nor embraced, explaining that she had become a fish and could never return to the land. Soon enough, she returned to the water, and, rejoining *Chipfalamfula*, she began to lament that she missed her family and wished to return to the land. As a kindly soul, *Chipfalamfula* agreed to release her to return to land, and to her family. Chichinguane stepped out of the water, still wearing her scales, and walked to the door of her mother's hut. When the two met, the scales fell to the ground, and there stood a human daughter.

Chichinguane, however, retained her alliance with Chipfalamfula and could command, or perhaps request his powers when she needed them.

One of the most curious monster tales is that of the Bride and the Monster, derived from a story told in the small southern African nation of Lesotho. This particular story concerns a beautiful young girl called Fenyane, who lived with her mother and little brother in a village beside a river. One day a messenger arrived on behalf of the chief of a neighboring village requesting Fenyane's hand in marriage for his son Sopo, to which the mother agreed. This was a great honor, and Fenyane's mother dug through her belongings to retrieve her own bridal accoutrements which she gave to her daughter.

Just then, some children ran into the village crying that Fenyane's little brother had fallen into the river, and hurrying off to see what the matter was, Fenyane's mother could not accompany her daughter to the neighboring village, but instead sent her on her way alone. As she made her way along the winding footpath between the two villages, Fenyane became aware of a whispering voice behind her. She knew that a person must never look back when leaving the village of their childhood, and so she walked on. The voice urged her to look back, for there was great trouble in her village. Her brother had been seized by the river spirits and her mother was so distraught that she had set fire to her huts.

"Look!" the voice urged. "And see for yourself."

For a long time, Fenyane resisted, but eventually, she could contain herself no longer, and she turned. There, standing on the path behind her, was *Moselantja*. *Moselantja* at one time commonly haunted the roads and byways of South Africa. While he looked human, his body was covered with scales, and a long tail protruded from his rear that had at its tip a mouth with small but very sharp teeth.

Having turned and observed him, Fenyane could not then be rid of *Moselantja*, and by the time the pair reached the village of her future husband, a handsome young man named Sopo, *Moselantja* had purloined all of Fenyane's bridalwear and was dressed in it himself. He then declared that he was Fenyane and that the unfortunate girl was simply his servant. He warned the family of the chief that his maid had a tendency to lie, and might claim to be Fenyane herself, but she was not to be believed.

He spoke in such a silky tone, and with such skill in mimicry that no one paid any particular attention to his odd appearance. Fenyane was so overawed that she did not dare speak a word, and while a little disappointed in the ugly girl his father had chosen for him, Sopo and *Moselantja* were duly married, and thus matters appeared settled. That night, Sopo and *Moselantja* retired to their wedding hut, and as the groom slept, the hungry tail of *Moselantja* slithered out to the celebration hall where the remains of the wedding feast were devoured. In the days that followed, the villagers were astonished that their store of meat and grain seemed nightly to disappear.

Fenyane, in the meanwhile, slept in the hut of a kindly, old woman who very quickly realized who Fenyane was and that *Moselantja* was an imposter. The old woman sought out the chief and his son and explained to them what had taken place, and moreover, she proposed a plan to outwit the evil *Moselantja*. A deep pit was dug, and after a day of cooking and preparation, the women of the village laid out at the base of the pit a lavish feast. When he laid eyes on the food arrayed at the bottom of the pit, *Moselantja* forgot his disguise immediately and slithered his tail down into the hole to begin devouring the food. Before long he had eaten so much he could barely move, and when all the food was gone, he turned over and went to sleep.

At a signal from the chief, the men leapt forward, and rolling *Moselantja* into the pit, they buried him. Later that day, while Fenyane's marriage to Sopo went ahead, the monster stirred in his grave, and within a few days, the first shoots of a pumpkin plant appeared above the ground. As the days passed, and after Fenyane announced her pregnancy, then a huge pumpkin appeared, growing larger every day. On the day that Fenyane gave birth, the pumpkin broke free and rolled into her hut and set upon her, beating her savagely. That night, Sopo hid in a dark recess of Fenyane's hut until the pumpkin appeared, at which he leapt upon it and stabbed it with his knife and then burned it to ashes in the fire.

A few days later, however, Fenyane's infant son developed a high fever and seemed likely to die until Sopo discovered a thorny pumpkin seed embedded in his flesh. Searching the hut, he discovered several more, and these too were promptly burned. When the ashes of the fire were finally cold, the little boy recovered, and peace returned to the village.

Online Resources

Other books about African history by Charles River Editors

Other books about African mythology on Amazon

Further Reading

Abimbola, Wade (ed. and trans., 1977). Ifa Divination Poetry NOK, New York).

Baldick, Julian (1997). Black God: the Afroasiatic roots of the Jewish, Christian, and Muslim religions. Syracuse University Press:ISBN 0-8156-0522-6

Barnes, Sandra. Africa's Ogun: Old World and New (Bloomington: Indiana University Press, 1989).

Beier, Ulli, ed. The Origins of Life and Death: African Creation Myths (London: Heinemann, 1966).

Bowen, P.G. (1970). Sayings of the Ancient One - Wisdom from Ancient Africa. Theosophical Publishing House, U.S.

Chidester, David. "Religions of South Africa" pp. 17–19

Cole, Herbert Mbari. Art and Life among the Owerri Igbo (Bloomington: Indiana University press, 1982).

Danquah, J. B., The Akan Doctrine of God: A Fragment of Gold Coast Ethics and Religion, second edition (London: Cass, 1968).

Gbadagesin, Segun. African Philosophy: Traditional Yoruba Philosophy and Contemporary African Realities (New York: Peter Lang, 1999).

Gleason, Judith. Oya, in Praise of an African Goddess (Harper Collins, 1992).

Griaule, Marcel; Dietterlen, Germaine. Le Mythe Cosmogonique (Paris: Institut d'Ethnologie, 1965).

Idowu, Bolaji, God in Yoruba Belief (Plainview: Original Publications, rev. and enlarged ed., 1995)

LaGamma, Alisa (2000). Art and oracle: African art and rituals of divination. New York: The Metropolitan Museum of Art. ISBN 978-0-87099-933-8. Archived from the original on 2013-05-10.

Lugira, Aloysius Muzzanganda. African traditional religion. Infobase Publishing, 2009.

Mbiti, John African Religions and Philosophy (1969) African Writers Series, Heinemann ISBN 0-435-89591-5

Opoku, Kofi Asare (1978). West African Traditional Religion Kofi Asare Opoku | Publisher: FEP International Private Limited. ASIN: B0000EE0IT

Parrinder, Geoffrey. African Traditional Religion, Third ed. (London: Sheldon Press, 1974). ISBN 0-85969-014-8 pbk.

Parrinder, Geoffrey. "Traditional Religion", in his Africa's Three Religions, Second ed. (London: Sheldon Press, 1976, ISBN 0-85969-096-2), p. [15-96].

Peavy, D., (2009)."Kings, Magic & Medicine". Raleigh, NC: SI.

Peavy, D., (2016). The Benin Monarchy, Olokun & Iha Ominigbon. Umewaen: Journal of Benin & Edoid Studies: Osweego, NY.

Popoola, S. Solagbade. Ikunle Abiyamo: It is on Bent Knees that I gave Birth (2007 Asefin Media Publication)

Soyinka, Wole, Myth, Literature and the African World (Cambridge University Press, 1976).

Alice Werner, Myths and Legends of the Bantu (1933). Available online at sacred-texts.com

Umeasigbu, Rems Nna. The Way We Lived: Ibo Customs and Stories (London: Heinemann, 1969).

Free Books by Charles River Editors

We have brand new titles available for free most days of the week. To see which of our titles are currently free, click on this link.

Discounted Books by Charles River Editors

We have titles at a discount price of just 99 cents everyday. To see which of our titles are currently 99 cents, click on this link.

www.ingramcontent.com/pod-product-compliance
Lightning Source LLC
Chambersburg PA
CBHW080854160726
47999CB00009B/3122